Secret Santa

Surprise

Quinn,

I hope you have
a very Merry Christmas!

Dec. 2016

From,
Miss Gatti

Ready, Freddy!

#1: Tooth Trouble
#2: The King of Show-and-Tell
#3: Homework Hassles
#4: Don't Sit on My Lunch!
#5: Talent Show Scaredy-Pants
#6: Help! A Vampire's Coming!
#7: Yikes! Bikes!
#8: Halloween Fraidy-Cat
#9: Shark Tooth Tale
#10: Super-Secret Valentine
#11: The Pumpkin Elf Mystery
#12: Stop That Hamster!
#13: The One Hundredth Day of School!
#14: The Camping Catastrophe!
#15: Thanksgiving Turkey Trouble
#16: Ready, Set, Snow!
#17: Firehouse Fun!
#18: The Perfect Present
#19: The Penguin Problem!
#20: Apple Orchard Race
#21: Going Batty
#22: Science Fair Flop
#23: A Very Crazy Christmas
#24: Shark Attack!
#25: Save the Earth!
#26: The Big Swing
#27: The Reading Race

2nd Grade

#1: Second Grade Rules!
#2: Snow Day Dare
#3: Secret Santa Surprise

Ready, Freddy!

Secret Santa Surprise

by ABBY KLEIN

illustrated by JOHN McKINLEY

Scholastic Inc.

To Rich,
The one who always made Christmas extra special!
Love you forever,
A.K.

ISBN 978-0-545-86357-5

10 9 8 7 6 5 4 3   15 16 17 18 19

Printed in the U.S.A.   40

First printing 2015

CHAPTERS

1. Ho, Ho, Ho! 9

2. Secret Santa Rules 17

3. Disaster! 29

4. Secret Spy Stuff 38

5. Super-Secret Spies 48

6. Surprise! 58

7. Great Idea! 68

8. Ho, Ho, Ho! Merry Christmas! 77

Freddy's Fun Pages 89

I have a problem.

A really, really big problem.

My class is doing Secret Santas.

We pick someone's name out of a hat,

and then we have to make a special

gift for that person. I picked the

worst name of all!

Let me tell you about it.

CHAPTER 1

Ho, Ho, Ho!

"What's for dessert, Mom?" I asked as I shoveled the last spoonful of mashed potatoes into my mouth.

"Slow down, Freddy," said my mom. "I don't want you to choke."

"And don't talk with your mouth full," said my sister, Suzie. "I don't want to see what you're eating. It's disgusting!"

I opened my mouth and stuck out my tongue

at Suzie. "AAAAAAAA!" Little bits of potato slipped off my tongue.

"EWWWW! EWWWW! EWWWW!" Suzie screamed, covering her eyes. "You are so gross!"

"Freddy," said my dad. "That's enough!"

"Where are your manners?" asked my mom. "You are acting like an animal!"

"Yeah," said Suzie. "Like a P-I-G, pig."

"Oink, oink," I snorted, and laughed.

"Really, Freddy," said my dad. "If you don't stop right now, then you won't be having any dessert."

"And mom made chocolate pudding," said Suzie.

I froze. "Did you say 'chocolate pudding'?"

"Yes," said my mom.

My eyes got big, and I started bouncing around in my chair. "Can I have it with whipped cream? Can I? Can I?"

"Not if you keep fooling around."

I stopped bouncing, sat up in my chair, and folded my hands in my lap. I looked over at my mom and grinned a big, wide grin.

"Much better," said my mom.

"Oh please," said Suzie. "Are you really going to fall for his 'I'm so cute' look?"

I smiled even wider.

"Take your dinner dishes to the sink while I get out the dessert," said my mom.

Suzie and I picked up our dishes and started walking toward the sink. "Unbelievable," Suzie mumbled.

"Works every time," I whispered.

I put my dish in the sink and sat back down. My mom got the pudding out of the refrigerator and put it on the table.

I grabbed it and began dumping huge spoonfuls into my bowl.

"Whoa, whoa, whoa," said my dad. "Slow down there. Leave some for the rest of us."

"But I LOVE pudding!" I said, licking my lips. "Especially chocolate."

"I think you have enough in your bowl," said my mom. "Pass it to your sister."

I passed the pudding to Suzie and jumped out of my chair.

"Now where are you going?" asked my mom.

"To get the whipped cream," I answered. "I have to have whipped cream on my pudding!"

I sprinted over to the refrigerator and galloped back to the table with the whipped cream can. I sprayed some on my pudding, and then I turned the can toward my face. Before my mom could say anything, I sprayed the whipped cream onto my chin to make a beard.

"Ho, ho, ho!" I said. "I'm Santa Claus."

A big glob of whipped cream slipped off my face and landed on the table. I started to lick it off with my tongue.

"Freddy!" my mom screamed. "What has gotten into you tonight?"

I put my hands on my belly and laughed again like Santa. "Ho, ho, ho! Merry Christmas!"

"Your Christmas won't be so merry if you don't behave," said my dad. He wasn't laughing. In fact, he looked pretty angry. He pointed toward the sink. "Go wash off your face. Now!"

I quickly washed off my face and sat back down.

"Really, Freddy," said my mom. "Why are you acting so crazy tonight?"

"Tonight?" said Suzie. "He acts crazy *every* night!"

"Well, he is being especially crazy tonight," said my dad.

"Sorry. I'm just really excited," I said.

"About what?" asked my mom.

"My class is going to do Secret Santas," I said.

"No way!" said Suzie. "I always wanted to do that."

"I know," I said. "Me, too."

"My teachers never did that. You are so lucky you got the new teacher, Miss Clark."

"Tomorrow we get to pick a name out of a hat," I told everyone. "Then we make something special for that person."

"That sounds like fun," said my mom.

"I'm so jealous," said Suzie.

Wow! I thought to myself. *Suzie is never jealous of me!*

"I can't wait!" I said. "I'm going to be Josh's Secret Santa, and I'm going to make him a snow globe with a surfer in it."

"Hold on there," said my mom. "I thought you told us you had to pick a name out of a hat."

I nodded. "You do."

"Then how are you so sure you're going to pick Josh's name?"

I smiled. "I just have this feeling," I said.

Suzie laughed.

"What's so funny?" I said.

"Oh, nothing. Nothing." She laughed again.

"Why are you laughing?" I demanded.

"I just thought of something."

"What? What did you think of?"

"What happens if you get Max?" she said.

"What?"

"What happens if you pick Max's name tomorrow?"

I stared at her for a minute. I hadn't thought of that. "That won't happen," I said.

"How are you so sure?" she said with a big grin on her face.

Because it can't happen, I thought to myself. *It just can't.*

CHAPTER 2

Secret Santa Rules

The next morning our classroom was buzzing with excitement. "Okay, everyone," said Miss Clark. "Sit down at your desks. I want to tell you about Secret Santas."

"This is going to be so cool," said Jessie.

"I know," I said. "I've always wanted to do Secret Santas. It sounds like so much fun!"

"I hope I pick your name, Freddy," said Josh.

"And I hope I pick yours," I said, laughing.

"That would be awesome if we picked each other," said Josh.

"Well, guess what? I know *I'm* going to pick Josh's name," said Chloe, fluffing her bouncy red curls and smiling in Josh's direction.

"No you don't!" shouted Max.

"Yes I do," said Chloe.

"Oh no you don't!" Max repeated. "It's totally random."

Chloe stood up and crossed her arms. "I just know I'm going to pick his name. I have this feeling."

"You're crazy," said Max, tapping Chloe on the head.

"Hey, don't touch me," Chloe whined as she swatted Max's hand away.

He tapped her head again. "Cr-aaaa-zy!"

"Stop it right now, Max, or I'll . . . I'll . . ."

"You'll what?" Max asked, grinning.

"I was wondering the same thing," Josh whispered to me. "What is *she* going to do to *him*?"

"Nothing," Jessie said, laughing. "She couldn't hurt a fly!"

"OOOOOOOO!" Chloe howled, and stamped her foot.

"All right, you two," said Miss Clark. "That is enough. You both need to sit down in your seats."

"But . . . but," Chloe stammered, her hands on her hips.

"But . . . but," Max said, imitating her.

That just made her even angrier.

"Did you hear that, Miss Clark? He's copying me!"

"He's copying me," Max repeated.

"You're so rude!"

"You're so rude!" Max mimicked again.

"He does a pretty good impression of her," Josh whispered to me.

"He's had a lot of practice," I whispered back.

"Max," said Miss Clark. "You are being very rude right now. It is not polite to imitate other people."

"That's right," said Chloe. "It's not polite."

"Please apologize to Chloe."

Max stared at Chloe, but he didn't say anything.

"Max, I asked you to tell Chloe you are sorry."

"Sorry," Max mumbled.

"You need to look at her and speak a little bit louder. I don't think she heard you," said Miss Clark.

"I'm waiting," said Chloe, tapping her foot on the floor.

"Sorry!" Max said.

"Okay, now sit down, both of you," said Miss Clark. "And stop wasting our time."

"That's one thing they're both really good at," Jessie whispered. "Wasting time."

"I know you're all excited about the Secret Santas," Miss Clark continued. "But before we pick names, I want to tell you a few rules."

"I am going to buy my secret person a million presents," Chloe blurted out.

"Well, that's the first rule," said Miss Clark. "You can only give your secret person one present on Friday."

"One present? One present? That's ridiculous!" said Chloe. "Then I'm going to get the most expensive present ever!"

"That's rule number two," said Miss Clark. "You can't buy anything for the person you pick."

"You can't buy anything? What do you mean?" said Chloe. "I don't get it. How do you give someone a present if you can't buy anything?"

"Did she really just ask that?" Jessie said to me. "She is unbelievable."

"Maybe she's an alien from another planet," Josh said with a chuckle.

"We are going to be *making* gifts for one another," said Miss Clark.

"Making gifts?" said Chloe. "I never *made* anyone a gift before."

Jessie rolled her eyes. "There's a first time for everything."

"You'll see," Miss Clark said, smiling. "Making gifts is really fun!"

"Are there any other rules?" Josh asked.

"Yes," said Miss Clark. "Do not wrap the gift you make. Just put it in the brown bag I'll be giving you today."

"A brown bag?" said Chloe. "That's so ugly and plain!"

"I want everyone's gift to look the same," said Miss Clark. "I don't want the wrapping to be a clue about who your Secret Santa might be. I want it to be a total secret. That's part of the mystery!"

"I love mysteries!" said Jessie.

"Me, too!" I said.

"Won't people be able to tell who gave them the gift by looking at the handwriting on the card?" asked Josh.

"Good point!" I said. "That's thinking like a detective!"

"I already thought of that," said Miss Clark. "So the name you pick out of the hat today is actually a sticker. You will stick that on the outside of your bag. When you bring your gift in on Friday, keep it in your backpack until you get into the classroom. Then give it to me as soon as you get in the room. That way no one will see the name on the bag."

"You really did think of everything," said Jessie.

"I tried," Miss Clark said.

"Can we pick now?" Chloe asked.

"I think we are just about ready. Any more questions?"

"What if we don't like the name we pick?" said Max. "Can we trade for somebody else?"

Of course I was thinking that, too, but I would never say it out loud!

"No," said Miss Clark. "You cannot trade. We are all friends in this class, and in the spirit of the holidays, we can all do something nice for one another. If you don't think you can do that, Max, then you don't have to participate. What do you say?"

"No, no, I want to do it," said Max.

"All right, then," said Miss Clark. "It's time to pick."

My heart started beating a little bit faster.

Miss Clark pulled a red Santa hat out of her desk drawer and began walking around the room. "When you pick the name, don't say a word and keep a straight face. You wouldn't want to spoil it for your secret person."

As she got closer to me, I whispered to myself, "Come on, Josh. I hope I pick Josh."

"Okay, Freddy, it's your turn to pick."

I reached my hand into the hat and swirled the names around, trying to feel for just the right one. My heart was beating so fast I thought it was going to leap out of my chest.

I closed my eyes and picked.

Miss Clark moved on to the next person, and I slowly opened my eyes and looked at the name.

OH NO! OH NO, NO, NO!!!! I silently screamed in my head.

The name on the sticker said M-A-X. I had picked Max!

CHAPTER 3

Disaster!

I was miserable the rest of the day at school. I couldn't stop thinking about how I was going to have to make a present for the biggest bully in the whole second grade, the one person who was meaner to me than anyone else at school.

"Hey, what's wrong?" Robbie asked when he sat down next to me on the bus. "Did something bad happen today?"

I nodded. "Something really bad happened. It's a disaster!"

"Oh no! What is it? Are you okay, Freddy?"

Just then Max got on the bus and sat down in the seat behind us. "Are you okay, Freddy?" Max said, imitating Robbie. "The little baby looks like he's going to cry. Do you need your mommy?"

Ooooooo, he made me so mad! "Leave me alone," I mumbled.

Max leaned over the seat and put his face right in mine. I could feel his hot, stinky breath on my cheek. "What did you say, little baby?"

"Nothing," I whispered.

Max grabbed my shirt. "I know you said something, fraidy-cat. Now, tell me what you said!"

Josh tapped Max on the shoulder. "I'll tell you what he said."

Max turned to look at Josh.

"He said, 'Leave me alone,' so you'd better do that," said Josh.

"Or else what?" said Max, chuckling.

"Or else I'll really give you something to cry about," said Josh.

Max stared at Josh for a minute. Then he went to find another seat on the bus.

Josh squished into the seat next to Robbie.

"Wow! That was awesome!" I said. "Most kids can't stand up to that big bully. Everyone is afraid of him."

"And he knows that," said Josh. "That's why he can get away with what he does. He knows that most kids won't fight back."

"Why aren't you afraid of him?" I asked.

"Because he really isn't that scary," said Josh. "He just wants you to think he is. If more people started standing up to him, he wouldn't feel so powerful."

"I know you're right," I said. "He's just so much bigger than I am."

"Enough about Max," said Robbie. "Freddy, I still want to know what you're so upset about."

"I don't know if I can tell you," I said.

"What do you mean you can't tell me? I know I'm not in your class this year, but I'm still your best friend, right? Best friends tell each other everything!"

"And I'm your second-best friend, right?" said Josh. "So you can tell me everything, too."

"Josh, can you keep a secret?" I asked.

"Of course I can," Josh said. "I'm really good at keeping secrets."

"Okay, because this has to do with Secret Santas, and Miss Clark said we weren't supposed to tell anyone in the class whose name we picked."

"I promise I won't say anything," said Josh.

I put my arm around Robbie and leaned in close to him and Josh. "Guess whose name I picked today for Secret Santas?" I whispered.

"Who?" said Robbie.

"Take one guess."

"Chloe?" said Robbie.

"No! I wish. That would actually be better than the name I picked."

"Chloe? Better? Now you're talking crazy," said Josh. Just then his eyes got big and wide. "Oh no, you didn't!"

"Oh yes, I did!"

"No way!"

"Yes way!" I said.

"Uh, could someone please fill me in on what's happening here?" Robbie asked.

"Freddy picked Max as his secret person," Josh whispered.

"Max!" Robbie blurted out. "Are you kidding me?"

"Hey!" Max stood up in his seat. "Did one of you losers just say my name?"

"NO!" Josh yelled back. "You must be hearing things."

Josh put his hand over Robbie's mouth. "Shhhhhh! We don't want him to hear us talking about him. He's not supposed to know."

"Sorry!" Robbie whispered. "I just can't believe you picked *him*!"

"I know. Tell me about it," I said. "I was so excited to do Secret Santas. Now I don't even want to do it anymore."

"Come on, Freddy. It will still be fun," said Josh.

"Maybe for you, but not for me. I have to do something nice for the biggest bully in the whole second grade."

"What are you going to make him for a present?" asked Robbie.

"I don't know," I said, sighing. "I have no idea what kinds of things he likes."

"I have an idea," said Josh.

"You do? You know what Max likes?"

"No, I don't know what he likes, but I have an idea how we can find out."

"Really?" I said. "How?"

"We spy on him," said Josh.

"We do what?" said Robbie.

"We spy on him."

"How do we do that?" I asked.

"Do you know where he lives?" Josh asked.

"Yep. He only lives a couple of blocks from my house."

"This afternoon you, me, and Robbie can sneak over to his house and spy on him. We'll try to find out what kinds of things he likes to play with."

"That's a great idea!" said Robbie. "A spy mission sounds like a lot of fun!"

"What if he catches us spying on him?" I said. "Then we'll really be in trouble!"

"He won't catch us," said Josh. "We'll be super-secret spies. He'll have no idea we're even there."

"Come on, Freddy," said Robbie. "It will be an adventure. You love adventures!"

"Oh, all right," I said.

"Let's meet at Freddy's house in half an hour to make our super-secret spy plan," said Josh.

We high-fived each other.

"Half an hour. My house."

CHAPTER 4

Secret Spy Stuff

"Hey, Mom!" I yelled as I slammed the front door. "I'm home!"

My mom came running in from the kitchen. "Freddy, how many times have I told you not to slam the front door?"

"Sorry, Mom," I called over my shoulder as I started up the stairs.

My mom stopped me. "Slow down, mister. Aren't you going to tell me about your day?"

"Not right now, Mom. I don't have time. Robbie and Josh are coming over in a few minutes."

"They are?"

"Yep. And I've got to get ready."

"Ready? Ready for what?"

"Ummm . . . ummm . . . we're going to go build snow forts. I have to find my shark fin gloves."

"Don't you want a snack?"

"No thanks!" I ran up the stairs two at a time. "Just send Josh and Robbie up when they get here."

"Okeydokey!" my mom said.

I went into my room and sat down on my bed. I hit my forehead with the palm of my hand. "Think, think, think. What do spies need?"

I got out a pencil and a pad of paper and started to make a list when Josh and Robbie came racing in.

"Hey, Freddy," they said.

"Hey, guys."

"What are you doing with the pencil and paper?" Josh asked.

"I'm making a list of the spy stuff we're going to need."

"What do you have on the list so far?"

"Not much," I said. "Just one thing, a flashlight."

"A flashlight?" said Robbie. "We aren't going on a spy mission in the dark! We're going in the middle of the day!"

"That's true," I said, laughing.

"I know what we need," said Josh.

"What?"

"Binoculars!"

"Yes, great idea!" said Robbie. "Binoculars are the perfect tool for spying. Suzie has binoculars, right, Freddy?"

"Yeah, she got them last year for Christmas for when she goes bird-watching."

"Perfect," said Josh. "You can borrow hers."

"Well, ummm . . ."

"Well, what?" said Josh.

"Suzie doesn't usually let me borrow her stuff."

"We'll just borrow them for an hour and then bring them back. She'll never know."

"I guess so," I said. "I'll go look for them in her room while she's downstairs eating her snack."

I stopped at the top of the stairs and listened.
I could hear Suzie talking to my mom in the
kitchen, so I tiptoed into her room and looked
in her closet. I didn't see the binoculars there,
so I quietly opened one of her dresser drawers.
I started rummaging around inside the drawer
when I felt a tap on my shoulder. "AAAAHHH!"
I screamed, and jumped about three feet in
the air.

"Surprise!" Suzie said.

"Suzie, what are you doing here?"

"I could ask you the same thing," she said. "What are you doing in *my* room? You know you're not allowed in my room without my permission."

"I was ummm . . . I was ummm . . ." I stammered.

"You were what?" Suzie demanded.

"I was looking for your binoculars."

"My binoculars? What for?"

"For uh . . . for uh . . ."

"Come on, Freddy. Spit it out! I haven't got all day."

"I need them for a snowball fight this afternoon. We need them to spy on the other team."

"And you were just going to take them?"

"I was going to borrow them. I planned on putting them right back where I found them. So what do you say? Can I borrow them?"

"Sure!" said Suzie.

"Really?" I said. I couldn't believe it was going to be that easy.

"But it will cost you."

I knew it, I thought to myself. Nothing with Suzie was that easy.

"What do you want?" I asked.

"You have to clean up my room for a week," Suzie said, grinning.

"A week!"

"Yep. A week," Suzie said, holding up her pinkie for a pinkie swear.

"A week? Really? How about two days?"

"A week or nothing. Do we have a deal?" she said.

I really needed those binoculars. "Fine," I said as we locked pinkies. "I'll clean up your room for a week. Now can I have those binoculars?"

Suzie got out the binoculars and handed them to me. "Here you go," she said. "You'd better not break them!"

I grabbed them from her and dashed back into my room.

"What happened to you?" Robbie asked. "You were gone forever."

"Suzie caught me."

"Oh no!" said Robbie.

"Oh yes!"

"So we don't have the binoculars?" said Josh.

"No, I have them," I said. "It just cost me cleaning her room for a week."

"A week!" said Josh. "That's harsh. Your sister is tough."

"Tell me about it," I said.

"Well, at least we have our most important tool," said Josh.

"What else do we need?" I asked.

"I think we should bring a pencil and a little pad of paper so we can take notes," said Robbie.

"Okay. I've got that right here," I said, handing it to Robbie.

"Spies also have to wear gloves so they don't leave any fingerprints," said Josh.

"Since it's winter, we'll already have gloves on our hands," said Robbie.

"Oh yeah. I forgot," Josh said, laughing. "Coming from California, I'm still trying to get used to Christmas in the snow!"

"One last thing," said Robbie.

"What?" I asked.

"Josh and I are wearing our jackets with a hood to hide our faces. Make sure you also wear your jacket with a hood, Freddy."

"Wow! You guys think of everything!" I said. "You really are super spies."

"So what do you think?" asked Josh. "Are we ready, Freddy?"

"Ready!" I said.

The three of us put our hands together. "One, two, three, super spies!" we shouted. "Let's go!"

CHAPTER 5

Super-Secret Spies

We walked out of my house and headed down the street.

"Hey, guys," said Josh. "I have a joke for you."

"I love jokes," I said. "Go for it."

"What do you call a snowman in the summer?"

"What?"

"A puddle!"

"Ha, ha, ha!" I said, roaring with laughter. "That's so funny. Isn't it a good one, Robbie?"

"It is," Robbie said. "But remember, guys, we have to be really quiet. We don't want Max to hear us coming."

"That's for sure," said Josh. "He can never know we were spying on him. If he ever found out, we'd be in BIG trouble!"

"You can say that again," I said.

As we walked past Mrs. Golden's house, her dog, Baxter, came bounding off the porch and ran over to us. He was wearing a jingle bell collar that was jingling all the way.

"Hey, Baxter," I said. "Should we call you Santa Paws? How you doing, boy?"

Baxter jumped up and knocked me to the ground. Then he started giving me wet, slobbery dog kisses all over my face.

Josh and Robbie started laughing hysterically.

"Ha, ha, ha! More! Give him more kisses, Baxter!" Josh said.

Baxter kept on licking my face. "EWWWW!" I yelled. "I think he just stuck his tongue in my ear!"

"EWWWW! That's gross," Josh said, laughing.

I was able to wiggle myself free and stand up. "Sorry, boy, but we've got to get going. We have to complete our secret spy mission before it gets dark."

Baxter wagged his tail.

"See you later, boy," I said as I started to walk away.

Baxter barked and started to follow me.

"No, boy. Not today. You can't come with us today. You have to stay here."

Baxter whimpered.

"I know you want to come with us, but with that jingling collar, you'll make too much noise."

Baxter looked at me with his sad puppy-dog eyes.

"Oh, don't look at me like that," I said. "I'll tell you what. If we get done early enough, we can stop by your house on the way home and play fetch with you for a little bit. How does that sound?"

Baxter barked and wagged his tail.

"All right, then. You go back up on the porch, and we'll see you later."

Baxter barked again and ran back to the porch.

"Come on, guys," I called. "We can run part of the way there."

The three of us took off running. After sprinting two blocks, Josh asked, "Are we almost there?"

"Yep," said Robbie. "About another half a block."

"Then we'd better slow down," said Josh.

We stopped running and walked in silence the rest of the way.

When we got to the house next door to Max's, Robbie motioned for us to hide behind a big tree. We knelt down in the snow and huddled together.

"Okay, guys. Now what?" I asked.

"I don't think we can see enough from here," Robbie whispered, "so we're going to have to find another hiding place."

"But where?" I asked.

"I think I have an idea," said Robbie. "Follow me, but stay low to the ground."

We crawled out from behind the tree and crawled over to a bush that was growing right on the side of Max's house.

"In here," Robbie mouthed, and pointed.

Josh and I followed him in.

"I definitely think we'll be able to see a lot more from here," Josh whispered.

"Freddy, do you want the binoculars?" asked Robbie.

"Why?"

"You'll need to crawl to that window over there and peek in with the binoculars to see what you can see."

"Me? Why me?"

"Do you want me to do it?" Josh asked.

"Ummm . . . yeah," I said.

"Okay. No problemo," Josh whispered, giving me a thumbs-up.

That's what I love about Josh. He never calls me a fraidy-cat or makes fun of me if I am afraid to do something. He is a great friend.

I handed Josh the binoculars. He crept out of our secret hiding place and crawled along the side of Max's house. When he was underneath Max's bedroom window, he slowly stood up and peeked in the window with the binoculars.

I held my breath.

Josh watched silently for about two minutes, and then all of a sudden he dropped to the ground and crawled like crazy back to the bush where we were hiding.

"Oh no! Oh no!" Josh whispered.

"What?" Robbie and I asked.

"I think he may have seen me!"

I was about to scream, but Robbie put his

hand over my mouth before any sound could come out.

"Shhhhh," he whispered. "The last thing we want is for Max to know we're here."

"What do we do?" I mouthed.

"Should we try to make a run for it?" Robbie asked.

"I don't think we can make it without him seeing us," said Josh.

Just then we heard the front door slam shut.

The three of us froze.

My heart was beating so fast I thought it was going to pop out of my chest. *KA-THUMP, KA-THUMP, KA-THUMP.*

I grabbed Robbie's and Josh's hands and squeezed them really hard.

Max appeared from around the corner of the house carrying something in his hand.

"What's that?" I whispered.

"I think it's a hammer," Robbie whispered back.

"A hammer! Oh no! What's he going to do to us with a hammer?"

Max was headed straight toward us now. He was whistling and swinging the hammer.

I gulped. "This is it, guys," I whispered.

Max's footsteps got closer and closer, and my heart beat faster and faster.

I closed my eyes. "I can't watch," I said. "We're doomed!"

CHAPTER 6

Surprise!

Max was now one step away from the bush where we were hiding. I could hear his footsteps crunching in the snow. I squeezed Robbie's and Josh's hands tighter. I held my breath.

I knew we never should have tried to spy on the biggest bully in the whole second grade, I thought to myself. *Any second now he's going to find us, and then I don't know what he's going to do! He's crazy!*

Crunch, crunch. I heard one step and then another. My stomach flip-flopped. *Crunch, crunch, crunch, crunch, crunch.* Wait a minute! I realized that Max had walked right past us. I opened my mouth to say something, but Robbie put his hand over my mouth again.

Josh lifted his finger to his mouth to signal me to be quiet.

We listened for Max's footsteps to get farther and farther away, and then Robbie took his hand off my mouth.

"Whew! That was a close one!" Josh whispered.

"Too close!" I said.

"I thought for sure he was going to find us," said Robbie.

"Me, too!" I said, letting out a huge sigh.

"If he wasn't coming after us, then where is he going?" Josh asked.

I shrugged my shoulders. "I have no clue."

"Should we peek out and see?" asked Josh.

"I'll peek," said Robbie. Robbie slowly pushed a bit of the bush aside and looked out.

"What do you see?" I asked.

"Nothing yet. Hey, Josh, hand me the binoculars."

Josh gave the binoculars to Robbie. "It looks like he's walking to the back of his yard."

"Really?" I said. "What's back there?"

"It's hard to tell. Oh, wait! It looks like he's opening a door."

"Opening a door?" said Josh.

Robbie adjusted the binoculars so they zoomed in closer. "Yeah. He just opened the door to a little shed."

Λ chill ran up my spine. "I don't think I want to know what's in that shed," I said.

"Maybe he's doing some weird science experiments," Robbie said.

"Maybe he's creating his own Frankenstein monster," said Josh, laughing.

"Don't laugh," I said. "I wouldn't be surprised if he was creating some kind of monster to scare the pants off all of us!"

"Seriously, Freddy," said Josh, patting me on the back. "Sometimes you freak yourself out way too much. You've got to relax, dude."

"Robbie, can you see what Max is doing in there?" I asked.

"I'm trying," said Robbie.

"Hurry up!" I said. "I want to get out of here before Max comes out of that shed."

"OH . . . MY . . . GOODNESS!" said Robbie.

"What? What is it?" asked Josh.

"It's a monster, right?" I said. "I told you guys he's creating a monster."

"No! It's not a monster, Freddy."

"It's not?"

"No, it's something way cooler!"

"Really?" Josh said. "Max is actually doing something cool?"

"Here, take a look for yourself," Robbie said, handing the binoculars to Josh.

Josh took the binoculars and put them up to his eyes. "HOLY COW!"

"My turn," I said, grabbing the binoculars from Josh. "Let me see."

"WOW! That *is* awesome!"

"I know, right?" said Robbie.

"I can't believe it. It looks like he's building a whole village."

"It looks just like those little villages people set up around their train sets at Christmas time," said Robbie.

"He's got houses, and stores, and a post office, and all kinds of stuff," said Josh.

"Do you think he built the whole thing by himself?" I asked.

"It looks that way," Josh said.

"Well, now we know what he needed the hammer for," I said, laughing.

"This is a total surprise," said Robbie. "I never expected to discover this when we decided to spy on Max."

"You can say that again," I said. I put the binoculars back up to my eyes. "This is what he must do every day after school."

"I guess it's like his big secret," said Josh.

"Oh no!" I gasped.

"What?" Robbie asked.

"He just looked this way. Do you think he knows we're here?"

"We're hiding in a bush. He can't see us!" said Josh.

"Maybe he can hear us," I said.

"I don't think so, Freddy," said Josh, laughing.

"He's still staring in this direction," I whispered nervously.

"He's probably just thinking," said Robbie. "I sometimes stare off into space when I'm thinking about something."

"Well, I don't want to take any chances," I said. "As soon as he turns back around, we need to make a run for it."

"We can't make a run for it," said Josh.

"Why not?" I asked.

"Because we are spies," said Robbie. "Spies move very slowly and quietly and do not make any noise at all!"

I looked through the binoculars one more time. "He's looking the other way! Now's our chance! Come on!"

"Wait, Freddy, first put the binoculars away," said Josh. "You wouldn't want to lose them."

"That's for sure!" I said. "I'd probably have to clean up Suzie's room for the rest of my life!" I carefully put the binoculars into my jacket pocket.

"Ready?" Robbie whispered.

"Ready!" we both said, giving a thumbs-up.

Robbie motioned for us to follow him. "Stay low to the ground."

We practically slid out of the bush on our bellies and crawled quickly along the side of Max's house. When we got to Max's front yard, we took off running like we were being chased by a bear, and we didn't stop until we were safely back at my house.

CHAPTER 7

Great Idea!

That night at dinner Suzie said, "So? Who's your secret person for Secret Santas? Didn't you pick the names today?"

"I was wondering the same thing," said my mom, "but you ran right upstairs when you came home from school, so I didn't get to ask you."

"Did you pick Josh like you thought you were going to?" asked my dad.

"No."

"Ha! Told you so," said Suzie.

I glared at her.

"Did you pick Jessie?" asked my mom.

"I wish. But no."

"I know who he picked," Suzie said grinning.

"You do?" said my mom.

"Yep," said Suzie. "Just look at Freddy's face. Does he look happy?"

"Not really," said my mom.

"That's because he picked Max. Right, Freddy?"

I didn't answer.

"Right, Freddy?" Suzie repeated.

I nodded my head slowly.

"So why do you look so upset?" said my dad.

"Because now the whole Secret Santas thing is ruined!" I whined. "I don't even want to do it anymore!"

"Freddy," said my dad. "Where is your Christmas spirit?"

" 'Tis the season of happiness and joy," said my mom.

"Well, I'm not feeling very happy right now," I said.

"You need to change your attitude," said my dad. "Right now you have a really *bad* attitude."

I hung my head and continued pouting.

"Your teacher is organizing this really special thing for all of you, and you just want to whine and complain," said my mom, "because you didn't pick your best friend's name out of the hat."

"I would have been fine with *anyone* else, just not Max!"

"Come on, Freddy," said my dad. "Max is a kid just like you."

"Not really. He's mean to everyone. He's the biggest bully in the whole second grade!"

"I know he's not always kind," said my mom, "but maybe if kids did more nice things for him, he'd start to change."

"This is your chance to do something nice for him," said my dad.

"Let's turn that frown upside down," my mom said, reaching over to draw a big smile on my face with her finger.

"I know how to make him smile," said my dad. He reached over and tickled me in the ribs. I tried to hold back from laughing.

"Oh . . . oh . . . I think I see that smile coming . . . there it is right there," my dad said, poking my cheek. He tickled me one more time, and I burst out laughing.

"Much better," said my mom. "Christmas is

a time of joy and laughter, not whining and pouting."

"So what are you going to make for him?" asked Suzie.

"I don't know," I said. "I had a ton of ideas for Josh, but I don't have any for Max."

"Well, what does he like?" my mom asked.

I shrugged my shoulders. "I'm not really sure." I said. "I think he likes to build stuff."

"Really? Like what?" said my dad.

"Little toy houses and cars, stuff like that."

"How do you know that?" asked Suzie.

"I uh . . . I uh . . ." I stammered. I had to think fast. I didn't want them to know that I had been spying on Max. "He brought one of the cars in for show-and-tell one day."

"Well, that's pretty cool," said my dad.

"Yeah, I guess it is," I agreed.

"I think I have an idea of what you could make for him," said Suzie.

"What?"

"Since he likes to build so much, why don't you make him a toolbox to keep all of his tools in?"

"That's a great idea!" I said.

"I know," Suzie said smiling. "I'm full of great ideas."

"That is a really good idea," said my mom. "It is a very thoughtful gift."

"I think Max will like that a lot!" I said.

"I'm happy to help you build it," said my dad. "When does it have to be finished?"

"We don't have a lot of time," I said. "We are going to be giving each other the presents on Friday, so we only have four days."

"No problem," said my dad. "I think I have some scrap pieces of wood in the garage left over from when I built the fence. We can use some of those pieces to make the toolbox."

"Great! When can we start?" I asked.

"We can start tonight right after dinner if you want," my dad said.

"Oh boy! Really?" I said, bouncing around in my chair. "That would be awesome! Thanks, Dad." I picked up my spoon and started shoving the rest of my peas into my mouth.

My mom grabbed my hand and stopped it in midair. "Freddy, we talked about this last night," she said. "You need to eat slowly. You are going to choke on those peas! You are holding a spoon, not a shovel."

"I just want to get done so Dad and I can get started on the project."

"I understand that," said my mom, "but you need to finish your dinner first without gobbling."

"The project can wait five minutes," my dad said.

I scooped up the last spoonful of peas, chewed them quickly, then washed them down with a big gulp of water. "Okeydokey! I'm ready to get started," I said, jumping out of my chair.

"I need about another ten minutes," said my dad.

"I don't think I can wait that long!"

"I'm glad you're so excited," said my mom. "That's a big change from a few minutes ago when you didn't even want to do Secret Santas."

"Tell you what, Freddy," said my dad. "Why don't you go down to the basement and start getting things set up. I'll meet you down there when I'm done."

"Okay, Dad!" I said as I headed out of the kitchen. "Hurry up. Don't take too long!"

"I won't," he said, laughing.

" 'You better watch out . . . you better not cry . . . you better not pout . . . I'm telling you why . . . Santa Claus is coming to town,' " I sang as I disappeared down the basement stairs.

CHAPTER 8

Ho, Ho, Ho! Merry Christmas!

When my alarm clock rang on Friday morning, I leaped out of bed, threw on my clothes, brushed my teeth, and raced downstairs.

"Wow! You're up bright and early," said my mom.

"I know. Today's the big day!" I said.

"You mean today is the day you stop being so annoying?" said Suzie.

"Ha-ha, very funny. No, today is Secret Santas day!"

"Oh, that's right," said my mom.

"Do you have the present?" asked my dad.

"Oops! I almost forgot it," I said, laughing. "I've got to go back upstairs and get it."

I ran up the stairs two at a time, grabbed the toolbox from my room, and flew back down the stairs.

"Got it!" I yelled as I skidded back into the kitchen.

"Do you want me to help you wrap it?" asked my mom.

"No thanks, Mom. Miss Clark said that kids might be able to figure out who their Secret Santa is by the way the gift is wrapped, so we are just supposed to put it in a brown paper bag."

"Sounds like Miss Clark has really thought about this."

"Yes, she has. She even made a name sticker to put on the bag so that kids can't try to figure out the handwriting."

I pulled the brown bag out of my backpack, gently put the toolbox inside, then stuck the sticker that said MAX on top.

"All set!" I said, and smiled. I put the gift into my backpack.

"I don't think you're all set," said Suzie.

I frowned. "Why not?"

"You don't look like Santa."

"Of course I don't look like Santa," I said, laughing. "I don't have a beard or a belly like a bowl full of jelly!"

"You need a Santa hat," said my mom.

"Great idea!" I said. "The only problem is I don't have one."

"Suzie does. She got one last Christmas."

"Can I borrow it? Can I? Can I?"

"I don't know," said Suzie.

"I'll take really good care of it! I promise."

"Come on, Suzie, let your brother borrow your hat for one day."

"Oh, all right. Just for today."

I threw my arms around her and gave her a great big hug. "You are the best sister ever!" I said.

"I know," said Suzie. "Don't you forget that."

Suzie went up to her room and came down carrying the fuzzy red hat with the big white pom-pom. She plopped it on my head. "There, now you look like Santa."

I patted my belly. "Ho, ho, ho! Merry Christmas!"

"All right, Old Saint Nick. You'd better eat

your breakfast or you're going to be late for the bus," said my mom. "I made you something special this morning — gingerbread pancakes."

"Gingerbread pancakes! That sounds awesome!" I said, licking my lips. "That's probably what Mrs. Claus makes for Santa's breakfast. Can I put whipped cream on them?"

"As long as you don't use it to make another beard!" said my mom.

I sprayed on a mountain of whipped cream, gobbled up three gingerbread pancakes, and dashed off to catch the bus. When Josh got on, we both started laughing.

"Nice hat, dude," said Josh, pointing to my Santa hat.

"Yeah, nice hat," I said, pointing to his Santa hat.

Max stood up and yelled, "Look at the little twinsies. Aren't they so cute in their fuzzy hats?"

"Sit down, Max," said Jessie. "You're just jealous that you don't have a cool hat like that."

Max looked at her. Then he sat back down.

"Jessie, you rock," said Josh.

Jessie smiled.

The bus pulled up to school, and we all raced off.

"Have fun!" Robbie called after us.

"Thanks! We will!" Josh and I yelled back.

When we got into the classroom, we all secretly gave Miss Clark our gifts.

"I just can't wait!" Chloe squealed. "This is

going to be so exciting! My nana got me this outfit just for today."

She had on a Santa hat, a matching red velvety dress with furry white trim, and shiny black party shoes.

"Watch me, everybody!" said Chloe.

"Do we have to?" Josh whispered.

"Do we have a choice?" said Jessie.

Chloe started twirling around the room and almost crashed into Max's desk.

"Hey, ding-a-ling! Watch where you're going!" yelled Max.

"I'm doing a dance from the famous ballet *The Nutcracker*."

"*You* are a nutcracker!" Max said, chuckling.

"No I'm not!"

"Yes you are!" said Max.

Miss Clark stepped in between the two of them. "Really? I'm surprised at the two of you. This arguing is ridiculous! It stops right now, or you both can skip the whole Secret Santas celebration. Do you understand me?"

Oh no! I thought to myself. *If Max misses the celebration, then he won't get my present!*

Chloe nodded. "Yes, Miss Clark."

"Max?"

Max nodded. "Yes, Miss Clark."

"Good. Now everybody come to the rug. We're going to pick numbers out of my Santa hat, and that will determine what order we will go in to open gifts. If you pick number one, you go first, number two, you go second, and so on."

"I'm going to go first," said Chloe.

"How do you know?" said Josh. "We haven't even picked yet."

"I just know," Chloe said, smiling at Josh.

I turned to Josh and whispered in his ear, "I think she likes you."

Josh just shook his head. "No way, dude!"

Miss Clark walked around with the hat so we

could pick our numbers. "Okay, now everybody open up your paper to see what number you got."

Max jumped up, pumped his fist in the air, and yelled, "I got number one! I got number one!"

"That's not fair," Chloe whined.

"It's very fair," said Miss Clark. "We picked out of a hat. It was totally random. Chloe, you just have to wait for your turn."

"I don't think she knows what the word 'wait' means," said Jessie.

"Or the word 'turn,'" said Josh.

Miss Clark handed Max his present. "Here you go, Max. This is from your Secret Santa."

My heart started beating like crazy. *What if he doesn't like it?* I thought to myself. I tried not to show any emotion on my face. I didn't want to give my secret away.

Max pulled the toolbox out of the bag. He just stared at it.

Oh no! I thought. *He hates it! He really hates it!*

All of a sudden, a big smile spread across his face. "This is awesome!" he said. "I've never had a toolbox of my own. This is one of the best presents I ever got!"

Merry Christmas, Max, I thought to myself. *Merry Christmas!*

Freddy's Fun
Pages

SANTA CLAUS FACE

Do you like Santa as much as Freddy does? Try making this adorable Santa Claus to hang on your front door for Christmas.

YOU WILL NEED:

flesh-colored construction paper
red construction paper
cotton balls
two googly eyes
a small pink pom-pom
a red marker
scissors
glue

DIRECTIONS:

1. Cut a circle out of the flesh-colored construction paper to make the face.

2. Cut a Santa hat shape out of the red

construction paper and glue the bottom of the hat to the top of the flesh-colored circle.

3. Glue one cotton ball at the tip of the hat and a line of cotton balls along the bottom of the hat.

4. Glue a bunch of cotton balls along the bottom and sides of the face to make Santa's beard.

5. Glue two googly eyes on the face.

6. Glue on a small pink pom-pom for the nose.

7. Cut a cotton ball in half and glue a piece above each eye to make eyebrows.

8. Cut another cotton ball in half, stretch it apart, and glue it under the nose for a mustache.

9. Draw a red smile under the mustache.

HO, HO, HO!

RED-AND-WHITE SLIME

Are you doing Secret Santas at your school? Try making this special holiday slime for your secret person!

YOU WILL NEED:

clear washable glue

white washable glue

liquid starch

water

red food coloring

a measuring cup

4 bowls and 2 spoons

DIRECTIONS:

1. In one bowl mix:
   ½ cup of water
   ½ cup of CLEAR glue
   a large amount of red food coloring

2. In another bowl measure out ½ cup of liquid starch.

3. Slowly mix the glue into the starch with a spoon and then mix it with your hands for a while. Let it sit.

4. Now mix:

    ½ cup of water

    ½ cup of WHITE glue ONLY (NO red food coloring!)

5. In another bowl measure out ½ cup of liquid starch.

6. Slowly mix the glue into the starch with a spoon and then mix it with your hands for a while. Let it sit.

7. After about an hour, your slime is ready to be played with (or wrapped up to give away as a gift)!

Have fun making pretend candy canes, Santa hats, Christmas cookies, or anything else you can think of!

CHRISTMAS JOKES

Here are some of Freddy's favorite
Christmas jokes to tell your friends!

Why does Santa have three gardens?
    He likes to HOE, HOE, HOE!

What is Santa's favorite candy?
    Jolly Ranchers

What do you get when you cross an apple with
a Christmas tree?
    A pineapple

What goes "Oh, oh, oh!"
    Santa walking backwards

What do Santa's elves learn at school?
    The ELFabet

Have you read all about Freddy?

Second Grade!

Don't miss any of Freddy's funny adventures!